Símbolos de nuestro país / Symbols of Our Country

Canto el himno nacional
I Sing the
"Star-Spangled Banner"

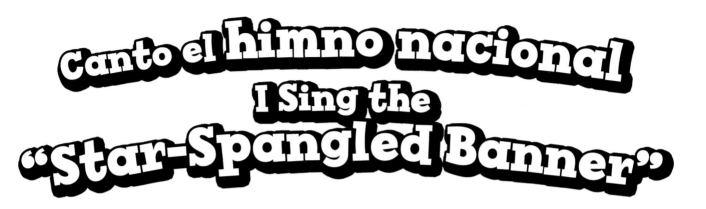

Devon McKinney

traducido por / translated by

Eida de la Vega

ilustrado por / illustrated by

Aurora Aguilera

PowerKiDS
press

New York

Published in 2017 by The Rosen Publishing Group, Inc.
29 East 21st Street, New York, NY 10010

First Edition

Translator: Eida de la Vega
Editorial Director, Spanish: Nathalie Beullens-Maoui
Editor, English: Caitie McAneney
Book Design: Michael Flynn
Illustrator: Aurora Aguilera

Cataloging-in-Publication Data

Names: McKinney, Devon, author.
Title: I sing the star-spangled banner = Canto el himno nacional / Devon McKinney.
Description: New York : PowerKids Press, 2017. | Series: Symbols of our
  Country = Símbolos de nuestro país | In English and Spanish | Includes index.
Identifiers: ISBN 9781499430523 (library bound book)
Subjects: LCSH: Star-spangled banner (Song)–Juvenile literature. | National
  songs–United States–History and criticism–Juvenile literature. |
  Flags–United States–History–19th century–Juvenile literature.
Classification: LCC ML3561.S8 M4 2017 | DDC 782.42/15990973–dc23

Manufactured in the United States of America

CPSIA Compliance Information: Batch #BW17PK: For Further Information contact Rosen Publishing, New York, New York at 1-800-237-9932

Contenido

Contents

Me encanta la clase de música.
Hoy vamos a aprender
"The Star-Spangled Banner".

I love music class. Today we're going
to learn "The Star-Spangled Banner."

4

Mi maestra dice que esta canción es especial.
¡Es nuestro himno nacional!

My teacher says this song is special.
It's our national anthem!

Un himno es la canción de una nación.

Las personas lo cantan en eventos importantes.

An anthem is the song of a nation.
People sing it at important events.

9

He escuchado esta canción antes.
¡Se canta antes de comenzar los
juegos de béisbol!

I've heard this song before. People
sing it before baseball games!

11

¿Qué significa su nombre?

"Star-Spangled Banner" es el nombre que se le da a la bandera de Estados Unidos.

What does the title mean?
"Star-Spangled Banner" is another
name for the American flag.

Mi maestra nos explica que la canción fue escrita hace mucho tiempo. Su autor era poeta.

My teacher says the
song was written a
long time ago.
The writer was a poet.

El poeta quedó atrapado en un barco durante una batalla. Desde allí, observó la batalla durante muchas horas.

The poet was trapped on a boat during a battle. He watched for many hours.

17

18

Hasta que al fin, el poeta vio la bandera de Estados Unidos ondear sobre un fuerte. ¡Eso quería decir que habían ganado los estadounidenses!

Then, the poet saw an American flag flying above a fort. That meant the Americans won!

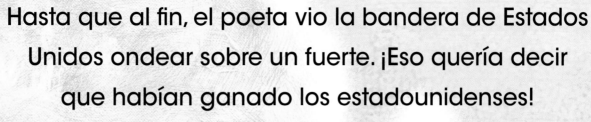

El himno de "Star-Spangled Banner" nos cuenta la historia de esa gran batalla. ¡Lo cantamos con orgullo!

20

The Star-Spangled Banner tells the story of that great fight. We sing it proudly!

21

Me encantó cantar nuestro himno nacional.
¡Quiero enseñárselo a mis amigos!

I loved singing our national anthem.
I can't wait to teach it to my friends!

Palabras que debes aprender
Words to Know

(la) bandera de
Estados Unidos
American Flag

(el) barco
boat

(el) fuerte
fort

Índice / Index

24